The Cow That Went OINK

by

Bernard Most

HARCOURT BRACE & COMPANY

Orlando Atlanta Austin Boston San Francisco Chicago Dallas New York
Toronto London

This edition is published by special
arrangement with Harcourt Brace & Company.

The Cow That Went OINK by Bernard Most.
Copyright © 1990 by Bernard Most.
Reprinted by permission of
Harcourt Brace & Company.

Printed in the United States of America

ISBN 0-15-300312-X

4 5 6 7 8 9 10   059   96   95   94

The illustrations in this book were done in Pantone
 markers on Bainbridge board 172, hot press finish.
Composition by HBJ Photocomposition Center,
 San Diego, California
Color separations were made by Bright Arts, Ltd.,
 Hong Kong.
Printed and bound by Tien Wah Press, Singapore
Production supervision by Warren Wallerstein and
 Michele Green
Designed by Alex P. Mendoza

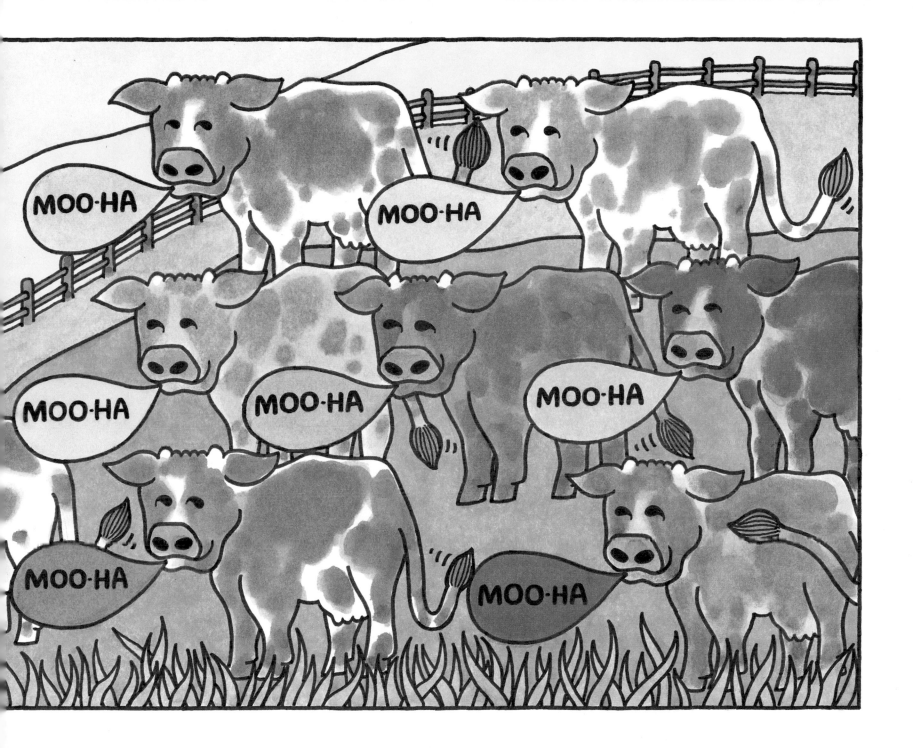

And the other animals on the farm laughed at her, too.

The cow that went OINK was very sad.

One day she heard a friendly MOO.

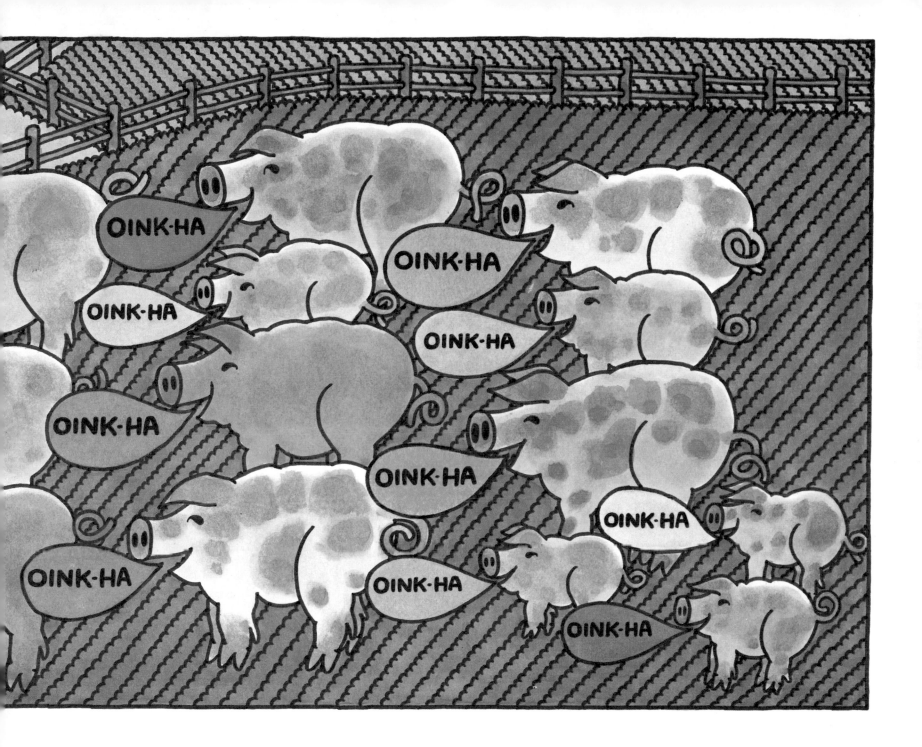

The pig that went MOO was very sad.

The cow that went OINK had an idea.
She would teach the pig to OINK.

So the cow that went OINK made a loud OINK, while the pig that went MOO listened carefully.

Then the pig that went MOO
tried to go OINK.

The horse, the donkey, and the sheep thought this was very funny.

But the pig that went MOO didn't listen to them. She listened to the cow.

And the pig that went MOO tried again . . .

and again . . .

and again . . .

until she finally went OINK.

The pig could OINK. Now she would teach the cow to MOO.

The cow that went OINK tried to go MOO.

The rooster, the turkey, and the duck laughed and laughed.

But the cow didn't listen to them.
She listened to the pig.

And the cow that went OINK tried again . . .

and again . . .

The cow and the pig were very happy.
Each of them could MOO and OINK.

And they were the only animals on the farm that could do both. So they had the last laugh.